This book belongs to:

....

....

....

For Our Turtle Dream Team

Amy, Amelia, David & Brett

RHH & TF

A BRUBAKER, FORD & FRIENDS BOOK,
an imprint of The Templar Company Limited

First published in the UK in hardback in 2011 by Templar Publishing
This softback edition published in 2013 by Templar Publishing,
Deepdene Lodge, Deepdene Avenue, Dorking, Surrey, RH5 4AT, UK
www.templarco.co.uk

First softback edition

ISBN 978-1-84877-665-4

Printed in China

Turtle and Me

ROBIE H. HARRIS

Illustrated by

TOR FREEMAN

B‖F‖&‖F

BRUBAKER, FORD & FRIENDS

AN IMPRINT OF THE TEMPLAR COMPANY LIMITED

I met Turtle on the day I was born.
On that great and important day, I was totally
tiny and Turtle was way bigger than me.
Now I'm way bigger than Turtle. But that doesn't matter.
We're best friends. We've been together forever.

Way back when I was a little baby,
every time I put my arms
around Turtle, I smiled.

And every time
I rubbed Turtle's tummy,
I laughed.

Back when I was
a bigger baby, I *had* to
have Turtle around.

But as soon
as I could
hold Turtle,

Every single time
Mummy left the room,
I yelled *Waaaaaaah!*

I stopped yelling.
Holding Turtle made me
feel okay again.

When I was still a little child and had to take
a nap, sometimes I felt lonely and sad.
But as soon as I snuggled up with my soft and
cuddly Turtle, I didn't feel lonely or sad any more.

Turtle's a lot older now.
And so am I. But I still
like to have Turtle around.

And sometimes I still
like to hold Turtle.
But now Turtle's colours
aren't all that bright.
And Turtle's ripped, raggedy
and old. Some bad things
happened to Turtle.

When I was still quite little,
I dumped a whole bowl
of spaghetti on my head.
That gooey, slippery
spaghetti slid down my chin
and onto Turtle. And
the two of us had yucky
orange spots all over us.

Last year our puppy, Pooch,
chewed a giant hole right
in the middle of Turtle's shell.

This year after I ate a big piece of Mummy's birthday cake,
and the candy rose on top, and a huge scoop of
chocolate marshmallow honeycomb crunch ice cream,
I threw up all over Turtle.

When anything that bad happens
to Turtle, I feel so awful that
sometimes I even cry. And I bet
Turtle feels awful too.

But when bad things happen,
I always make sure that Turtle
gets sewn up, washed up,
fixed up – and is okay again.

TURTLE
REPAIR KIT

Last month I left Turtle at the park.
That was the worst! I thought I would
never ever see or hold Turtle again.
Mummy and I ran back to the park.
I cried the whole way.

But Turtle was still there!
At the bottom of the slide!
All covered with mud!
With gum on one foot!
And two new rips!

So I carried Turtle
all the way home,
even though Turtle felt
so-ooo grrr-oss.

Back home, we
tried to wash off
the icky-sticky
part and the slimy
muddy part.
But Turtle was
still grrr-oss.
So we sewed up
the rips, gave Turtle
a bath, and
put Turtle in
the dryer.

After all that,
I gave Turtle
the biggest hug.
And I decided
for sure that
I would never let
anything bad
happen to Turtle
ever again.

But then – the most worst thing of all happened.
Last Friday my friend and I sailed around the
world. Turtle was the Captain, so Turtle steered the ship.

But my friend said *she* wanted to steer the ship
and she grabbed Turtle from me. I said that Turtle was
still the Captain and I grabbed Turtle back.

Now Turtle had the biggest, baddest,

most gigantic, most horrible rip—ever!

"You ripped my Turtle!
You wrecked Turtle!" I yelled.
"Having Turtle's a BABY thing!"
yelled my friend.
"I'm not a baby! I'm a pirate!"
I yelled back.

"Well, I'm going home!"
yelled my friend.
And she did.

I held Turtle tight.

The rip was so big that
almost all the stuffing in Turtle's
tummy fell out.
"Oh-hhh, poor Turtle!" I cried.

And I stuffed the stuffing back inside
as fast as I could and taped Turtle's
tummy back together.

But now Turtle looked stupid.
So I left my ripped-up, stupid old
Turtle on the floor. I didn't
need Turtle any more.

At bedtime Daddy
brought me Turtle.
"But Daddy," I said, "I don't
want Turtle any more…"
"Okay," he said. "I'll put
Turtle back on the floor."

Mummy turned out the light.

I shut my eyes very tight.

I hugged my pillow.

I counted to seventy-seven.

I sang a song.

I
squeezed
my
eyes
tighter.
And
then
I
yelled,

Daddy came in. "Do you want Turtle?" he asked.
"NO!" I said. "Having Turtle's a baby thing!
And I'm BIG! And I'm getting bigger!
So I don't need Turtle
at all ever again!"

"You are very big now," said Daddy,
"but not *all* big. Not just yet." Then he grabbed
Turtle and flopped down on my bed. Daddy rubbed
Turtle's nose and pretended to snore.
That made me giggle.

Then I rubbed Turtle's tummy and pretended to snore.
And that made Daddy laugh. Even though I was so very
big now – holding Turtle still felt pretty good.
"Night-night, my big boy," whispered Daddy.

"Night-night, my Daddy," I whispered.
"And night-night, my good-old, chewed-up,
sewn-up, taped-up, ripped-up, raggedy Turtle."
And before I could count to thirty-three,
I fell asleep. And I think Turtle did too.